The Day the Earthworms... And their Friends...

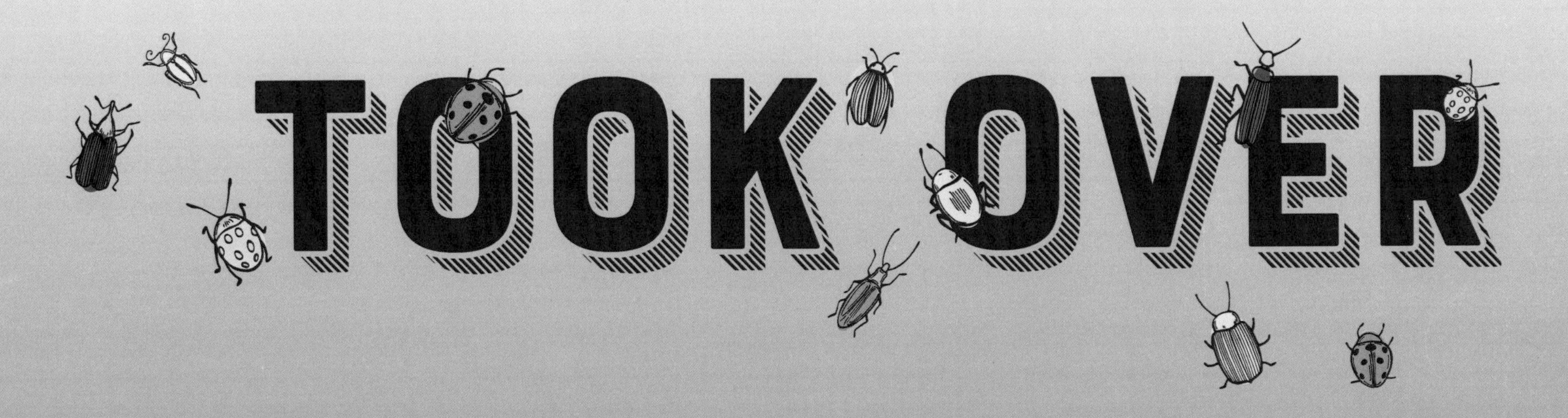

WRITTEN & DRAWN BY

JUDITH A. GORE SMITH

The Day the Earthworms… And their Friends… Took Over

First Edition

Hardcover: ISBN 979-8-8229-0867-3
Paperback ISBN: 979-8-8229-0868-0

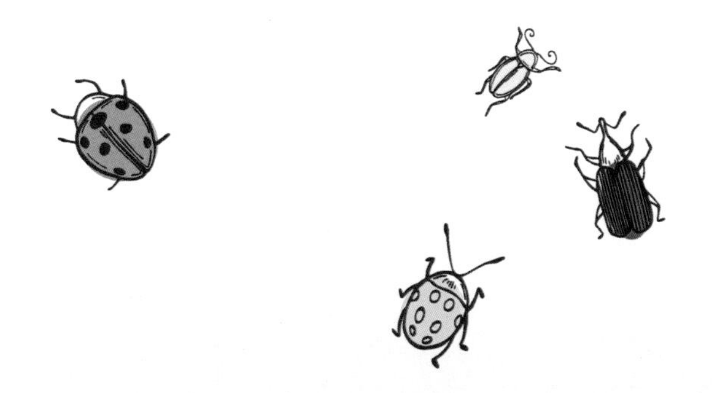

Dedication

I would like to dedicate my book to my Mother 👵...and my two children, Tim and Sue who grew up to be Industrious Earthworms in their own Fields. 🪱🪱My son 👦as a 📚🪱 Librarian and my daughter 👩as a Scientist.🔬

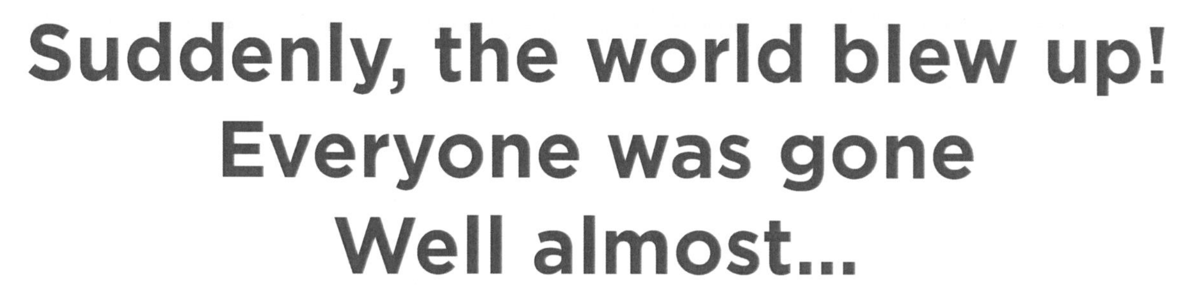
Suddenly, the world blew up!
Everyone was gone
Well almost...

WORLD HISTORY FOR

"Back in the year 2020 humans ruled the Earth and destroyed all of the trees, flowers, & animals
Oh! Show us Grandpa!

on the land and in the water

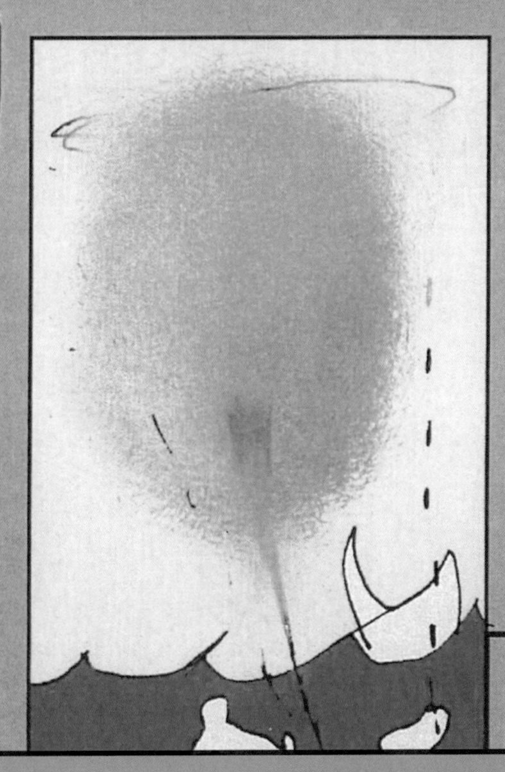

...until all was silent aboveground."
What's going on up there?

"And as all the creatures BIG and small came to the surface, they gasped and crowded together in shock. There was nothing to see for miles!"

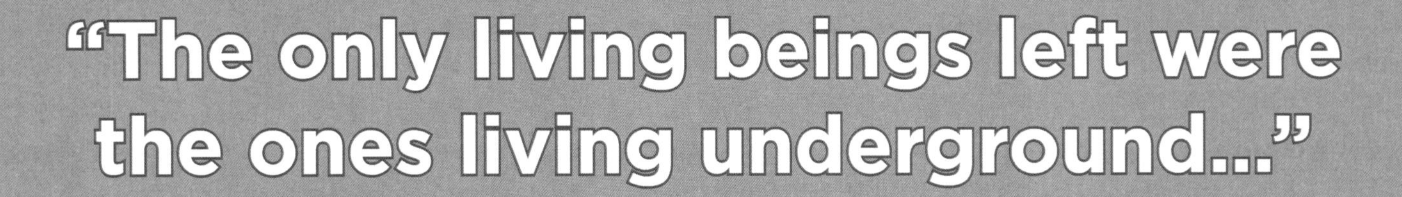

"And s-l-o-w-l-y they came up from their underground tunnels and looked around."

Really grandpa?!
Why were we friends?
Why did they
like us then?

Yes, little ones.
We were friends with the humans.
I believe they were called
fishermen and farmers.
Way cool grandpa!
Why did the
fisherman and
farmers like us?

Grandpa shrugged his shoulders. "I guess the humans thought we were inferior creatures and could use us as they wanted." The little ones blinked and looked at each other in shock.

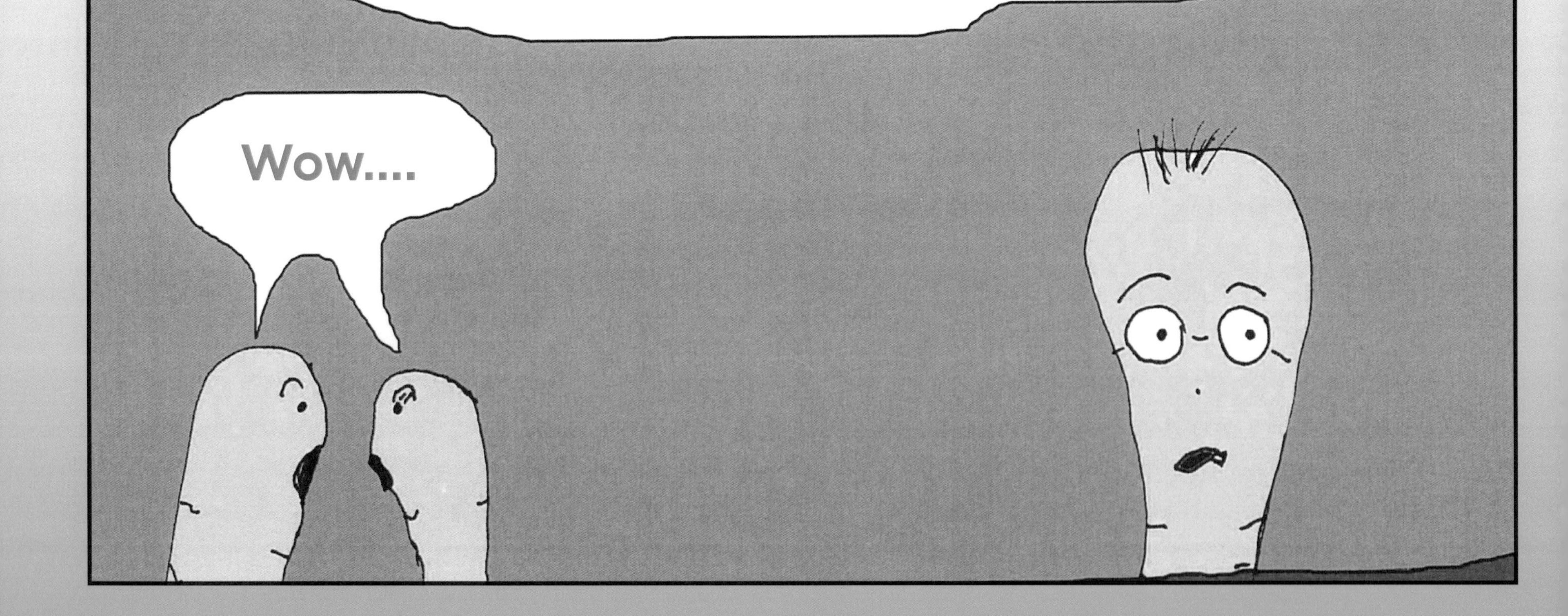

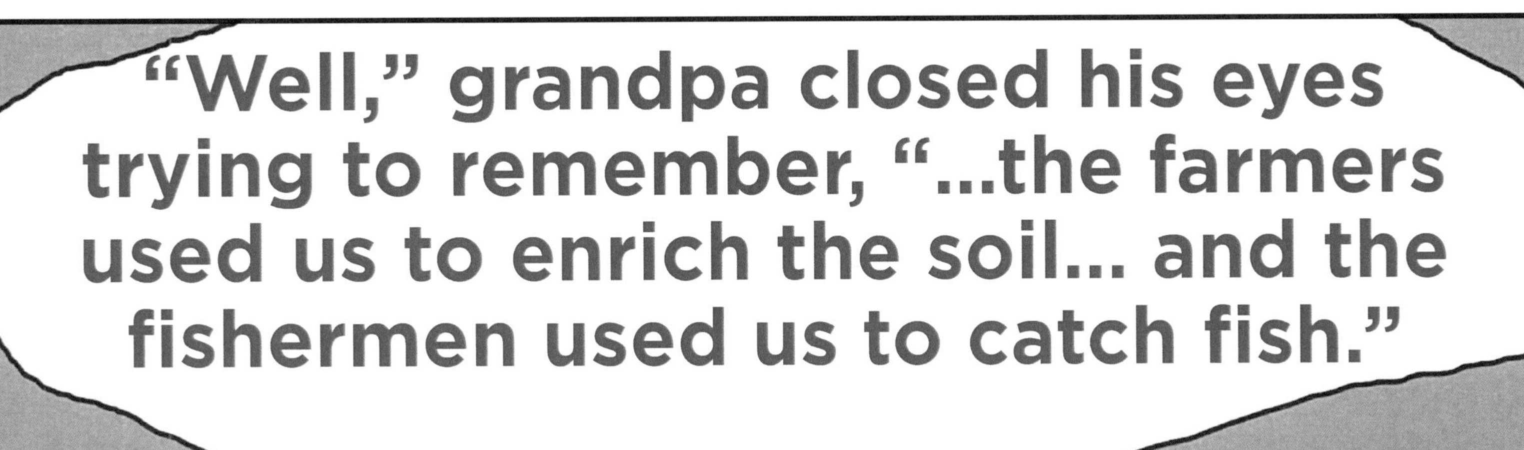
"Well," grandpa closed his eyes trying to remember, "...the farmers used us to enrich the soil... and the fishermen used us to catch fish."

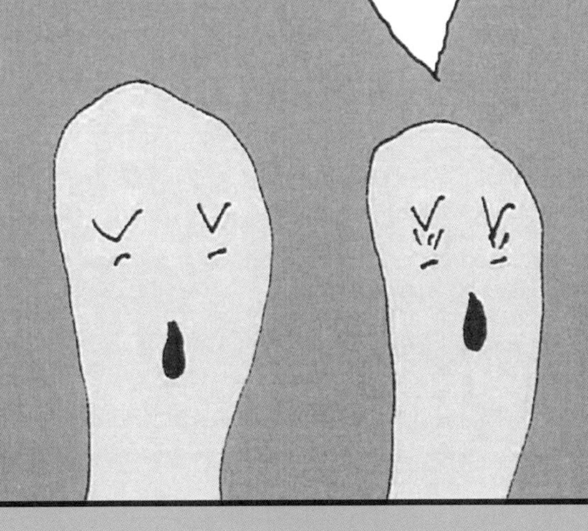
Oooh... ughh. That's really weird Grandpa!

And disgusting!

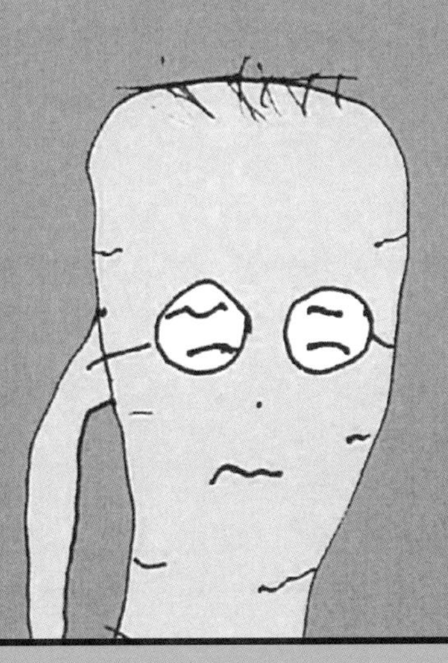

But Grandpa now the humans are all gone and We and our underground friends are the only ones left!

Yes... that is true little ones. I guess the humans thought they could destroy the Earth but still survive.
I guess they were not as intelligent as history tells us.

But why grandpa? Why did the humans destroy the whole world aboveground?
Grandpa sighed and put the book down...
WORLD HISTORY FOR

They didn't want to help the other creatures on and below the ground.
Suddenly the little ones began to cry and huddled closer.

The little ones yelled, "Will our underground world ever be destroyed?!"

Sadly grandpa closed the book and started to walk away.

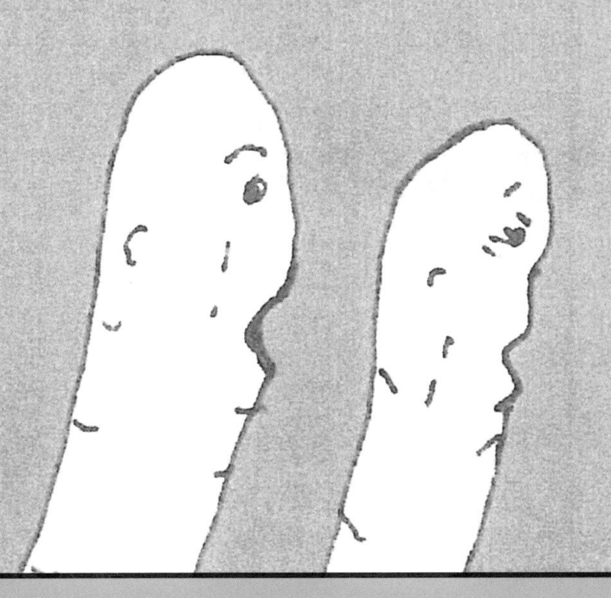

"Let's hope not but as long as we respect other creatures and try to do the right thing Mother Earth should let us live."

THE END

(of this story but hopefully not the world)

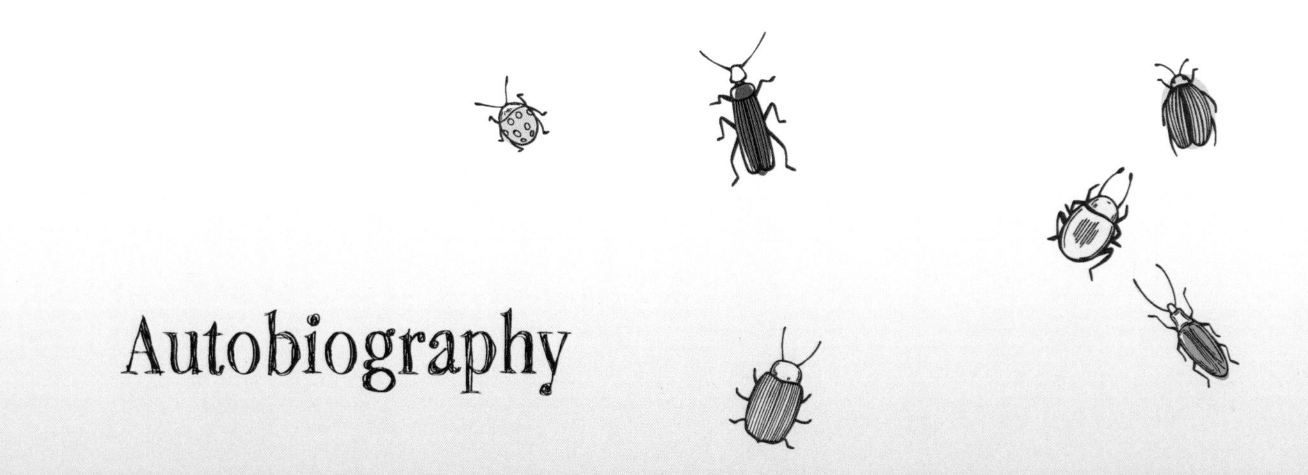

Autobiography

I have been writing ✍since I was a child. I think I first realized I had a talent for writing when I had a poem published in my High 📰 school Newspaper!
To my surprise my teacher made me read it in front of the class!!...

As years passed I tried various forms of writing ✍including short stories, poetry and even Plays...🎭..based in Nature both Fiction and Non-fiction..🌻🐍🐿🐛🦋🌼🌞!

I think I finally found my Niche in....👧👩🏫 Children's Literature and I even took a course in the subject. My greatest accomplishment as a writer is when I receive positive feedback from family 👨‍👩‍👦 and friends!🗣🌞👩🏫

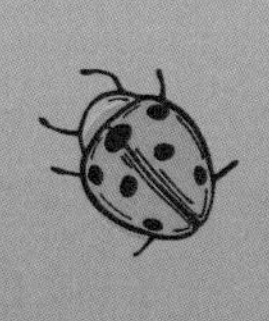

Lightning Source UK Ltd.
Milton Keynes UK
UKRC031244240223
417590UK00002B/13
* 9 7 9 8 8 2 2 9 0 8 6 8 0 *